Sometimes
I'm
Scared

This book is dedicated to all the children
who have learned not to be scared— JA & MN

For Oliver, we all get scared sometimes— BL

Published by

MAGINATION PRESS
An Educational Publishing Foundation Book
American Psychological Association
750 First Street, NE
Washington, DC 20002

For more information about our books, including a complete catalog, please write to us,
call 1-800-374-2721, or visit our website at www.maginationpress.com.

Printed by Worzalla, Stevens Point, Wisconsin

Library of Congress Cataloging-in-Publication Data

Annunziata, Jane.
Sometimes I'm scared / by Jane Annunziata and Marc Nemiroff ; illustrated by Bryan Langdo.
  p. cm.
ISBN-13: 978-1-4338-0449-6 (hardcover : alk. paper)
ISBN-10: 1-4338-0449-2 (hardcover : alk. paper)
ISBN-13: 978-1-4338-0550-9 (pbk : alk. paper)
ISBN-10: 1-4338-0550-2 (pbk : alk. paper)
1. Fear in children—Juvenile literature. I. Nemiroff, Marc. II. Langdo, Bryan, ill. III. Title.
BF723.F4A753 2009
155.4'1246—dc22   2008053623

10 9 8 7 6 5 4 3 2 1

Sometimes I'm Scared

by Jane Annunziata, PsyD
and Marc Nemiroff, PhD

illustrated by
Bryan Langdo

IMAGINATION PRESS
WASHINGTON, DC
American Psychological Association

Everyone is afraid sometimes.
It's normal.

There are lots of different things
that kids can be afraid of.

One thing kids can be scared of is the dark, because it's harder to see things clearly and how they really are. Everyone's imagination gets bigger at night.

Maybe you feel worried at night. One kind of night worry is that a robber will come into the house.

Kids might also worry about monsters in their rooms at night. But have you ever noticed that during the day there are no monsters in your room?

Remember this when you start to get scared at night!

There are also some things in nature that might feel scary to you.

Kids sometimes get afraid of things like loud thunder, bright lightning, strong winds, fast storms, big water, or fire.

These can seem too large, too fast, too loud, or just **too much**!

And sometimes your own feelings seem the same way. They can feel too big and out of control, and that really bothers kids.

Kids like to be the boss of things.
But some things you just can't control.
That's why big feelings might scare you.

Kids can also get scared when all of a sudden
they see something they were not expecting
or something that does not look very friendly.

It might be a big
barking dog,

a buzzing bee,

or a spooky spider.

These are bad surprises.
They make kids worry that they might get hurt,
even when they are just fine.
Kids only like good surprises!

Here's a different kind of thing that you might be scared of. Have you ever noticed how some kids are afraid of Santa Claus in the mall? Or a picture in a book that just doesn't look right?

And some kids are afraid of circus clowns.

These things are all the same in one way. They look strange and different! Most kids only like things that they know and that look regular to them. So when things don't look quite right, you might feel scared.

But good news!

There are a lot of ways to help
you feel not so scared.
You can

● Understand your feelings.

● Practice special breathing.

● Picture nice things.

● Pretend to be what scares you.

● Think encouraging thoughts.

● Change the way you think.

● Take little steps.

Understanding your feelings and why some things are scary helps.

Sometimes things really happen that make you afraid, but sometimes your own feelings bother you. When feelings bother you, they can make you worried or scared. Mad, sad, and frustrated feelings seem to bother kids the most. When your feelings bother you a lot, your imagination can make things scary.

Usually imaginations are for fun. They give you lots of new ideas when you play. But sometimes, when you are upset, your imagination stops being fun and starts turning safe things into scary things.

Let's say somebody pushes you down on the playground, and you feel very, very angry. And then, all of a sudden, you feel scared of buzzing bees on the playground when you weren't afraid of them before. Your imagination just made those bees scary because your angry feelings were bothering you.

Practicing special breathing is a good help, too.

This is how you do it:

1 Breathe in slowly
through your nose.
Fill your chest with air,
like it's a balloon.

2 Breathe out through your
mouth very, very slowly.

3 Do this slowly five times.
You'll begin to feel more relaxed.

Picturing nice things in your mind is another way to feel less scared.

For example, think of something you really like. Maybe it's a favorite place or a stuffed animal you really love. Or it could be anything else that makes you happy or helps you feel good.

When you think about something nice,
it sort of chases the scary thoughts away.
Doing the slow breathing and thinking
about something nice at the same time is
another good way to relax.

Pretending to be the very thing
that scares you sometimes helps,
too. Some kids worry that this is
a bad idea, but it can really help.

If dogs scare you, pretend that you are a big dog.
Have someone in your family pretend to be afraid.

Be sure to bark loudly!

Then walk on all your dog legs and show that you won't hurt anyone.

Thinking encouraging
thoughts helps a lot.
You can do this by talking to
yourself in a way that makes your
fears and worries smaller.

Here's an example:

When kids are afraid of thunderstorms,
they can tell themselves,

"Thunder is just a loud noise.
It can't hurt me.
It can only surprise me.
That's all."

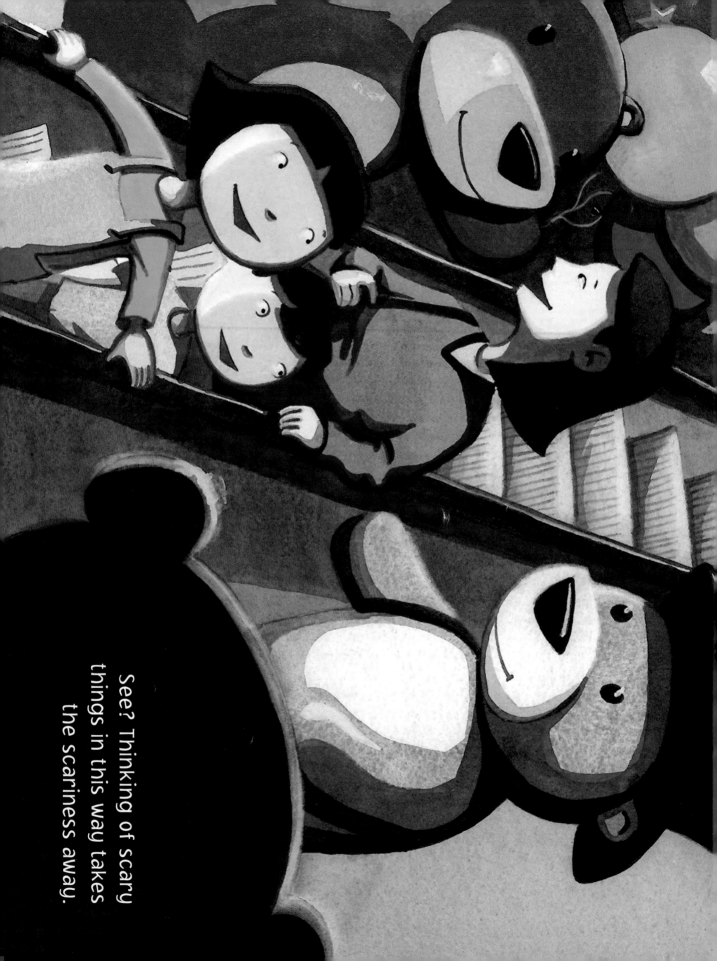

See? Thinking of scary things in this way takes the scariness away.

Changing the way you think helps, too.

Here is another example.

Some kids are afraid of escalators and elevators.

Instead of being afraid of them, kids can think,

"An elevator is just a room that goes up and down,

and an escalator is just stairs that move."

Taking little steps can help you. Practice getting used to the thing that scares you a little bit at a time, step-by-step.

Let's pretend that you are afraid of spiders. Your mom or dad can teach you to take little steps to help you get near something that scares you. You will feel less afraid if you do the special breathing when you take the steps.

Remember that moms and dads know a lot about understanding feelings and how imaginations work so they can be a big help, too!

And then you won't feel so scared.

Note to Parents

Many children experience situations causing anxiety, worry, or fear at various times through childhood. Children may fear the dark, insects, loud noises, big adults, barking dogs, or costumed characters. Perhaps you remember a time when Santa Claus or thunder and lightening frightened you?

While fears can be distressing to you and your children, it helps to understand that they indicate that your child has reached a developmental milestone, and has achieved a more sophisticated way of relating to the world. Certain fears are part of normal child development and are not only expected, but are actually desirable for your child. Nightmares, for example, are quite common in children three to five years old. This is because children at this age are in a peak period of conscience development: they have become more aware of the world around them and their imaginations and fantasy life have expanded. And kids begin to understand that bad things really can happen and that scary and dangerous things do exist. All this may cause fears.

Other fears can be signposts for parents. Fears let us know that our children are fretting and may need our help to express feelings they wish they didn't have. Other times, kids need help "processing" and understanding experiences or situations that are unfamiliar to them or that they are not quite ready to comprehend. Left alone, these feelings and experiences may be transformed into anxiety, fears, or worries. In this instance, understanding where fears originate can really help parents help their children.

Where do fears come from?

Over-generalizing. Consider this: your child is outside playing and a large dog comes running over and knocks her down. She gets upset and this causes her understandable fear and anxiety. But then your child becomes frightened and anxious about being near all dogs and might even become afraid of pictures of dogs or the sound of a dog barking. When this happens, it is called "over-generalizing." The fear and anxiety caused by the initial dog experience lead her to over-generalize and develop into her wanting to avoid all dogs, never having the opportunity to overcome her fear and to learn that most dogs are quite safe and friendly.

Uncomfortable feelings. Many fears come from inside your child and are often an expression of another feeling altogether. Those unexpressed feelings typically involve anger, disappointment, or negative thoughts toward a parent or sibling. Kids might worry that these feelings aren't "nice" or good to have. Because kids would rather not have these uncomfortable feelings, especially toward family members they love, they try to get rid of them by projecting their troubling feelings onto things in the real world. Essentially, they transform feelings into fears.

A child, of course, isn't aware that he's doing this. In his mind, he's afraid of dogs because they simply seem scary. He doesn't know that he really is bothered by his own "barking feelings" that seem too big and strong. His fear overpowers his knowledge and his parents' reassurance that the neighborhood dog that he's seen many times is friendly. This is actually a very common way that people of all ages deal with feelings that worry or bother them.

Unpredictable feelings. Other times kids can develop certain fears and anxieties when events are out of their control or unpredictable, reminding them of their own feelings and reactions (like anger or impulsive outbursts) that also seem unpredictable or out-of-control. One common fear of this type is thunderstorms. Your child might develop a fear of thunderstorms, in part because she is unsure when they might happen. And the heavy rain of thunderstorms can remind her of feelings that seem too strong or overwhelming. The loud boom of thunder and the flash of lightning can also remind her of strong angry feelings. Too much rain, too much noise, too much feeling, too uncomfortable!

Fear of "strange" things. Your child may also have certain fears that make absolutely no sense to you. You might think, Why would my child be afraid of Santa Claus at the mall? Or a clown at the circus? Or a drawing in a book? Simply put, young children can be scared of things that are unfamiliar to them and seem strange. Their minds aren't always ready to take in an image that seems so out-of-the-ordinary, and they become anxious. Young minds also often have difficulty making the switch from a picture of Santa Claus, for example, to a "real live" Santa Claus. The acceptable picture has become alive, and the child experiences this as just too much. This feeling of "just too much" might also extend to grown-ups dressed as witches or a clown at a birthday party. And often, a child might be frightened when he sees someone with a disability such as an artificial limb or an unusual facial feature such as a large birthmark or a lazy eye for the same reasons.

How you can help

Parents can help their children navigate their way through normal fears and worries. General reassurance and support is a good place to start. You can also help your child manage his anxieties by teaching him some simple coping techniques as described in the book. Working with your child little by little will empower him to take on and overcome his fears.

Understand your feelings. Because many fears are caused by feelings unknown to your child, you can start by addressing some of the most common bothersome feelings. This is a little like being an "emotions detective" but with a very light, non-intrusive touch. You might say, "Honey, are you so scared of the dark tonight because of that argument that you and your brother had?" Or "Jake, how come those bees over there got so scary right now? Usually they don't bother you when they're not near you. I wonder if something else is bothering you today." If Jake can't respond to your question, think back over the day to see if you can arrive at an educated guess and gently present that. You could then say, "Maybe you're upset because you're so mad at Scott for not playing with you? Let's talk about those feelings and maybe your bee-worry will go away."

Practice mindful breathing. All of us, including our kids, carry our fears and stress in our bodies. But by breathing slowly and purposely, you can teach your child to relax her body and quiet her anxious mind. You might teach your child to count the number of breaths as she does them: five in-breaths and five out-breaths. Concentrating only on breathing and counting diverts your child from thinking about her

fears while physically calming her down. Mindful breathing is an effective relaxation technique because it also is "subject-changing" in that it takes your child's mind off of her fears.

Picture nice things in your mind. Fears are often accompanied by scary visual images. Children can learn to visualize another "safe" or fun image to replace those scary scenes. For example, picturing a horse in a pasture or imagining playing at the beach replaces the negative, fearful image with a positive, relaxing one. As your child pictures the positive, it transports her away from her fear. This is an effective method for reducing fears for two reasons: First, it serves as another form of diversion from the fear. Second, it provides your child with a "mind-picture" that evokes the opposite feelings of fear. You can be particularly helpful by working with your youngster in advance to develop her positive imagery. Thus, she will have her positive mind-picture at the ready, to call upon when needed.

Pretend to be what scares you. Another way to help your child feel less at the mercy of his fear is to have your child pretend to be what scares him. He might get down on the floor and bark like a dog or run through the house like big gusts of wind or storm clouds. Children like this technique because it appeals to their sense of play even while incorporating the very thing that scares them. Because part of some fears involves the feeling of helplessness— "Something scary is going to happen to me and I don't know when and I can't stop it"—giving your youngster the opportunity to become the scary object or event empowers him and may really diminish his worry.

Think encouraging thoughts. "Self-talk" can be a very effective method for quieting fears and worries. It puts the child more in control of the scary situation and counters some of the negative and inaccurate thoughts that often accompany children's fears. Parents can teach their child how to talk to herself and what words she might use when she is confronting a scary situation, such as "I know I can do this. I'm going to be so proud of myself." You can also teach your child self-statements that are specific to her worry, like "Thunder is just a loud noise," or "This is a friendly dog that likes kids." Most of the